THE SIX CROWNS

TRUNDLE'S QUEST

THE SIX CROWNS

ALLAN JONES GARY CHALK

GREENWILLOW BOOKS
An Imprint of HarperCollinsPublishers

This book is a work of fiction. References to real people, events, establishments, organizations, or locales are intended only to provide a sense of authenticity, and are used to advance the fictional narrative. All other characters, and all incidents and dialogue, are drawn from the author's imagination and are not to be construed as real.

Trundle's Quest

Text and illustrations copyright © 2010 by Allan Frewin Jones and Gary Chalk

First published in 2010 in Great Britain by Hodder Children's Books, a division of Hachette Children's Books. First published in 2011 in the United States by Greenwillow Books.

The right of Allan Frewin Jones and Gary Chalk to be identified as the authors of this work has been asserted by them.

The text of this book is set in Transitional 521 Bitstream
Book design by Sylvie Le Floc'h

Library of Congress Cataloging-in-Publication Data
Jones, Allan Frewin, (date).
Trundle's quest / by Allan Jones ; illustrated by Gary Chalk.
p. cm.—(The Six Crowns)
"Greenwillow Books."
Summary: Trundle Boldoak's simple life as the town lamplighter is turned upside-down the night he meets Esmeralda, a Roamany hedgehog, who whisks him away on a quest to find six fabled crowns and fulfill his role in an ancient prophecy.
ISBN 978-0-06-200623-3 (trade bdg.)
[1. Adventure and adventurers—Fiction. 2. Prophecies—Fiction. 3. Badgers—Fiction. 4. Hedgehogs—Fiction. 5. Animals—Fiction.] I. Chalk, Gary, ill. II. Title.
PZ7.J67795Tr 2011   [Fic]—dc22   2010010341

11 12 13 14 15 CG/RRDB 10 9 8 7 6 5 4 3 2 1
First Edition

 Greenwillow Books

Six are they, the Badgers' crowns.

If power ye seek, they must be found.

Crystal, iron, and flaming fire—

Gather them, if ye desire.

Ice and wood and carven stone—

The power they give

Is yours

Alone.

$\mathcal{P}$ROLOGUE

The legends say that once—long, long ago—there was a single round world, like a ball floating in space, and that it was ruled over by six wise badgers. The legends also tell of a tremendous explosion, an explosion so huge that it shattered the round world into a thousand fragments, a vast archipelago of islands adrift in the sky. As time passed, the survivors of the explosion thrived and prospered and gave their scattered island homes a name—and that name was the Sundered Lands.

That's what the legends say.

But who believes in legends nowadays?

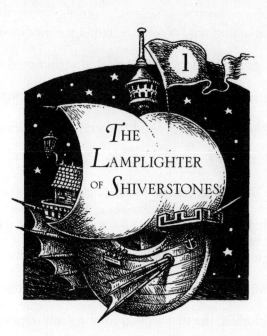

1

THE LAMPLIGHTER OF SHIVERSTONES

Trundle Boldoak smiled as he lifted his candlepole to light the final lamp of Market Square.

Evening was coming on fast, but Trundle's job was done—all the lamps of Port Shiverstones were burning now. From Docking Street to Gatherer's Turnpike, the yellow flames flickered behind their glass panels, illuminating the highways and thoroughfares of the small trading town.

Leaning on his candlepole, Trundle gazed up into

the darkening sky. Far away he could see the twinkling lights of the few islands that floated within eyeshot of Shiverstones. Beyond them, the darkness was sprinkled with the opening eyes of a hundred thousand stars.

"And now to home," Trundle murmured to himself as he headed across the Market Place. The end of his candlepole clicked sharply on the cobbles as he passed the great stone fountain with the granite statue of the founder of Shiverstones at its center. Furrowman Plowplodder, the first animal to bring cabbages to the flat, windswept island—farmer forefather of all the endless acres of cabbages that were now Shiverstones's principal crop.

Windships came here from far and wide, trading Shiverstones cabbages for earthenware pots and cast-iron pans, for candles and cheese and cloth and hoes, for buttons and buckets and boots and stoves, and for everything else the farmers and merchants of Shiverstones might need.

Trundle had spent all of his short life in Port Shiverstones, as had his parents and his grandparents before him. All his relations were dead now, and Trundle was quite alone, but he didn't mind that so very much. He had his work to do. The hereditary job of Lamplighter was not a glamorous or an exciting one, but it earned him ten sunders a day, which was enough for his simple needs.

"Good evening, Mistress Gleet. Good evening, Farmer Gossage," he called cheerily to passing townsfolk as he made his way toward Lamplighter's Lane and the small cottage that he called home.

"Good evening, young Trundle," they replied as they hurried along. "The wind's up tonight!"

It was always good to get out of the stiff, chill winds that blew across the land of Shiverstones. Even in high summer, through the toasty months of Greengrow and Beetime and Sunhover, the Shiverstones nights could be cold and bleak.

Now that Trundle had finished his evening rounds, he was looking forward to a cup of cabbageleaf tea and a warm bowl of cabbage broth. And then a quiet evening with his feet up and his snout in a good book.

He always went to bed early with his alarm clock set for dawn; by sunrise he needed to be busy with his snuffing staff, putting the lamps out again. Then he would spend the morning trimming the wicks and polishing the lamp glass and topping up the oil and happily passing the time of day with friends and neighbors. Yes, all in all, his was a good life, and he was contented with it.

He ambled down the center of Lamplighter's

Lane. The two yellow lamps above his front door flickered and danced as he approached, as if they were the eyes of the house, sparkling with joy to see their master returning.

He stepped onto the porch and lifted the latch. As he pushed the door open, he could already smell the broth that he had left warming over a low flame.

"Peace and quiet," he said happily, stepping over the threshold.

Suddenly he heard a swift patter of feet behind him. Before he even had time to glance over his shoulder, something hit him hard on the back, and he was sent sprawling forward across the flagstones of his parlor floor. He skidded helplessly, gathering rugs as he went, spluttering and gasping under a heavy weight that pressed down on his back and knocked all the breath out of his body.

He came to a halt with his snout almost in the hearth.

"You're smaller than I expected," said a voice. "And where's your sword?"

Breathless and befuddled, Trundle managed to squirm onto his back. A strange girl hedgehog sat squarely on his stomach, looking down at him with a critical gaze.

She had a mischievous face, grubby and unwashed, but enlivened by a pair of bright, flashing eyes. The shabby dress she wore might once have been a deep red color, but now it was so stained and dirty that it was more gray than anything else.

Trundle had never seen her before in his life.

"Get off me!" he gasped. "What are you playing at? Who are you?"

The girl clambered off and held out a helping paw. He scrambled up, ignoring the offer of assistance.

"I'm Esmeralda Lightfoot, the Princess in Darkness," she said cheerfully. "And you're the Lamplighter!"

"So what if I am?" Trundle said angrily. "That's no reason to jump on me like a Windrush hare!" He dusted himself off a little. "What do you want? Be quick. I'm busy."

"I want *you*," Esmeralda said. "Time's wasting. Come on, we have a windship to catch."

Trundle looked warily at her. The girl was clearly mad, but she needed careful handling. Now that he was on his feet and his brain was unscrambling, he noticed that her dress was Roamany. He'd never actually been face-to-face with a Roamany before—the romantic Roamany caravans never came to Shiverstones—but he had seen pictures of the Roamany folk in books. And he'd read about them, too; enough to know they were the only people in all of the Sundered Lands who had *magic* about them.

If this girl was Roamany, it wouldn't be wise to antagonize her—she might turn him into a carrot or

a cobblestone or a shred of thistledown. Apparently Roamanys could do things like that.

"I think you may have mistaken me for someone else," Trundle offered cautiously, edging toward the side of the fireplace, where he knew a stout iron poker could be quickly snatched up if the need arose.

"Not at all," Esmeralda said. She fumbled for a moment in a pocket in her dress and then brought out an oblong piece of wood, about two inches long by one inch deep. Trundle noticed that the block of wood had pictures carved on its four long sides. "This is a Badger Block, this is," she announced, holding the piece of wood up to Trundle's face. "See?"

"If you say so." Puzzled, he peered at the picture cut into the side facing him.

His eyebrows shot up. Carved into the wooden block was a picture of a hedgehog—a hedgehog dressed exactly as Trundle was dressed, a hedgehog with a Lamplighter's candlepole in one paw and a long sword in the other.

"Well?" Esmeralda insisted. "It's you, isn't it?"

Trundle opened and closed his mouth a couple of times, but could think of nothing useful to say.

"This is one of the magical and ancient Badger Blocks from the old times," Esmeralda explained. "You've surely heard of the powers of the prophetic Badger Blocks?"

"Um . . . no," said Trundle. "Not as such."

Esmeralda frowned at him. "That doesn't matter right now," she said. "The thing is, I picked this block from the black sack and it came up Lamplighter—and the Lamplighter is quite obviously *you*! I knew it the moment I saw you."

Trundle took a long, slow breath. "I have no idea what you're talking about," he said gently. "But if you tell me what you want, I'm sure I'll be able to point you in the direction of someone who can help you." By this he meant he wanted her out of his house and as quickly as possible, with a bolted door between them.

Esmeralda blinked at him. He got the impression she thought he was an idiot, which was rather annoying.

"When I was born," she began, "Aunty did a reading of the Badger Blocks and found that my picture was the Princess in Darkness. Everyone has a picture that relates to them, okay?"

Trundle nodded.

Esmeralda touched a paw to her chest. "I'm the Princess in Darkness." She pointed at him. "You're the Lamplighter. The two of us need to go and board a windship. We must follow the prophecy of the Badger Blocks and find the first of the Six Crowns of the Badgers of Power. *Now* do you understand?"

"The Badgers of Power?" Trundle scoffed, hardly able to keep from laughing. "They're not *real*! The stories about them are just . . . well, children's tales. You can't seriously believe . . . that . . . there . . . really . . . were . . ." His voice trailed off as he saw the girl looking more and more ferocious.

"The legends are absolutely real!" she said. "The badgers existed, and their six crowns still exist. And for some reason, *you're* needed to help find them." She shook her head. "Aunty once told me that the Fates sometimes use the most unlikely creatures to work their will." She eyed him up and down. "And for this task, the Fates have chosen *you*.

"Now then," she went on briskly, "gather whatever you think you might need on the journey, then let's get going."

"Going? Going where?" Trundle gasped.

"To the docks, to find a windship to take us to the first of the Six Crowns!" Esmeralda declared.

"Okay," Trundle said firmly. "This has all been very interesting, and I'm thrilled to have met you, but it's my dinnertime now, so if you don't mind . . ." He spread his arms and started to herd her toward the still-open front door. "Do send me a postcard to let me know how you're getting on," he added with a strained smile. "Address it to Trundle Boldoak, Lamplighter's Cottage, Lamplighter's Lane, Port Shiverstones." If necessary, he intended to give her a helpful shove out into the night before slamming the door on her and throwing the bolt.

"Now look here—" Esmeralda began.

But whatever she'd been planning on saying next was drowned out by a loud explosion that shook the little cottage and sent dust raining down on their heads.

Shocked, Trundle stared out into the night. A bloom of reddish cloud was rising behind the rooftops from the direction of the docks. Before he could catch his breath, there was another explosion, and then another and another.

Boom! Crash!

Boom! Crash!

BOOM! CRASH!

Trundle and Esmeralda stood together on the doorstep, staring into a night suddenly full of noise and smoke and leaping flames. Voices rang out—frightened voices, screaming and shouting and wailing—and there were other voices, too, harsh, guttural voices that whooped and howled and bellowed.

"It's Captain Grizzletusk!" Esmeralda gasped, her voice shaking. "We're too late! The pirates have found us!"

2

RAZORBACK AND THE PIRATES

Esmeralda's words made Trundle's heart almost stop. The people of Shiverstones didn't know much about the wide realms of the Sundered Lands, but even in this quiet backwater they had heard terrifying stories of Captain Grizzletusk, the pirate hog.

Esmeralda turned to Trundle, her eyes filled with fear. "We have to run!"

"We?" Trundle yelped. "What do you mean—we?"

"Here are your choices," Esmeralda said determinedly. "Either I stay here and Grizzletusk finds us—or we go before the pirates arrive." Her eyes narrowed. "You decide!"

Trundle stared at her.

A little while ago, he'd been looking forward to nothing more energetic than a bowl of broth and a good book, and now suddenly he had to choose between being chopped into pieces by a band of marauding pirates or fleeing his cozy home with a mad Roamany girl!

"I'm very sorry," he said, making a last desperate effort to hold on to his peaceful, sensible life, "but this is nothing to do with me." And so saying, he backed through the doorway and slammed the door on her.

Leaning against the wooden panels, he breathed hard, listening to the hideous din of the savage pirates. Pirates in Shiverstones! Even now he could hardly believe it. He had expected the crazy girl to yell for help and to hammer on the door, but there was no sound from her. After a few moments, he pressed his ear to the panels.

No. Nothing.

"Esmeralda?" he called tentatively. "Are you still there?"

"Yes," came a dull reply.

"Aren't you going to run away?"

"No."

He frowned. "Why not?"

"What's the point?" came Esmeralda's flat voice. "If you won't come with me, I may as well wait here to be recaptured."

Trundle closed his eyes and bumped his forehead against the door a couple of times, trying to dislodge the disturbing thought that was growing in his brain. The thought that he really ought to *do something to help her!*

With a deep sigh, he opened the door. Esmeralda leaped in with a wide grin on her face. "I knew you wouldn't let me down!"

Beyond her, at the dark end of Lamplighter's Lane, Trundle caught his first glimpse of the pirates. He didn't like the look of them one little bit. There were pigs and rats and weasels and foxes, all dressed outlandishly and armed with cutlasses and—worst of all—with muskets and smoking pistols.

"Is there a back way out?" Esmeralda asked, slamming the door shut and shooting the bolt. "Quickly, now—there isn't much time."

Nodding, Trundle led her across the parlor, through a door, along a corridor, through the scullery, and into the washing room. From here a door opened into his neat garden. Beyond the low drystone wall, endless acres of cabbages stretched out under the night sky.

Esmeralda stopped on the threshold. "You're sure you don't have a sword?" she asked.

"I'm positive," Trundle assured her.

"Not even hidden in the attic or under the floor-boards? One that might have slipped your mind?"

He stared at her. "Hardly."

"Then I expect we'll find it during the quest," she said with a nod. "But right now our problem is how to get off this benighted island without being caught by Grizzletusk and his cutthroats. They're hot on my trail!"

She sprinted across the garden with Trundle close behind, and in a moment the two of them were over the wall. The rows and rows of cabbages extended into the distance, looking weirdly unnatural in the starlight glow, like ranks of squat, blobby monsters brooding with evil intent.

Another explosion made Trundle jump. He looked back. The night sky was aglow with a ghastly red light, and he could hear gunshots in the town. In all of the Sundered Lands, only the pirates knew the secret of the exploding powder; only they wielded muskets and blunderbusses and flintlock pistols.

"Why are the pirates chasing you?" he asked.

"No time to explain," Esmeralda replied. "I'll fill you in later." She pointed across the fields. "Where does this lead?"

"This is all Farmer Pyepowder's land," Trundle told her. "The light you can see in the distance is his farmhouse. And beyond Farmer Pyepowder's land is Farmer Gidding's land, and beyond that is Farmer Stickleback's land, and—"

"I get the picture," Esmeralda interrupted him. She gestured toward the town. "Is this the only port?"

"Yes."

"So the only way to get off this dismal island is to go back to the docks," she said, rubbing her snout. "Hmm. Tricky!"

"We could hide in the fields," Trundle suggested, waving a paw toward the cabbage-filled horizon. "They'd never find us in there."

She looked at him with wide, solemn eyes. "Yes," she said, "they *would*. Come on, back into town. Sneaky's the word! They're dangerous and violent, but they're not very bright—except for the foxes, of course. We'll have to watch out for *them*." She climbed back over the wall and, keeping low, peered around the corner of the house into the lane.

Trundle considered his options. None looked good, and at least the girl seemed to have some idea

of what was going on. With a heavy sigh, he decided
to follow her.

"We need to get to the docks without being seen,"
Esmeralda whispered. "Got any ideas?"

"Yes, follow me," said Trundle. "I know every alley
and backstreet and passageway—I'll get us there."

Esmeralda smiled. "You're a good fellow,
Trundle," she said. The warm glow he felt on hearing
these words cooled somewhat when she added, "Even
though you are a bit dim."

With Esmeralda close on his heels, Trundle
slipped alongside his cottage and made a quick dash
for the cover of the long row of houses that formed
one side of Lamplighter's Lane.

It was very strange to be out and about so late,
and he might have been intrigued by the experience
had he not been terrified for his life. As it was, his
mouth was dry as bone, and an iron fist was squeezing
his stomach into a painful knot. He glanced at

Esmeralda; her eyes were narrowed and her face was grim, but he got the impression she was more excited than frightened. Maybe this kind of thing was quite normal to her.

Who *was* she? How had she talked him into this?

No time! Questions could come later. Staying alive and uncaptured was the important thing now.

As they dashed from cover to cover, Trundle could see the pirates looting and pillaging their way through the town. They were an ugly, ferocious bunch, sporting bloodred earrings and gold teeth that glittered when they grinned their evil grins. They poured through the town, smashing windows and kicking in doors, sending the terrified townsfolk scuttling for safety. And as they rampaged, they sang and hollered and filled the night with their cruel laughter.

Market Square was crawling with the horrible creatures, firing their muskets into the air, dancing in the fountain, and climbing all over the statue of

Furrowman Plowplodder. They had set fires in the lovely old buildings around the square so that the windows blazed with a grisly light and flames roared up through the roofs.

Trundle saw a group of terrified townsfolk being herded into the square. For a moment he stood in an archway, trembling with fury as he watched his friends and neighbors being poked and prodded by knives and swords and menaced by long, dreadful muskets.

"Empty your pockets, my lovelies," bellowed a great scarred hog with a long purple feather in his hat and a huge evil-eyed raven perched on his shoulder. "Pop all your precious things into the sacks provided by my merry mates. Come along now, don't be shy—let's be having your jewels and gewgaws. No donation is too small."

"Give till it hurts, my pretties!" croaked the raven. "Give till it hurts!"

"That's Razorback," hissed Esmeralda, standing at Trundle's side. "He's Grizzletusk's bosun, and one of the foulest hogs ever to walk a windship's deck. The raven's called Captain Slaughter, and he'd jab his beak in your eye soon as look at you. Where Razorback and Captain Slaughter ply their trade, Grizzletusk can never be far behind."

At that moment, a pirate rat turned his long, loathsome snout in their direction. His eyes glittered with malice. "Join us," he squealed, gesturing with his pistol. "Don't be shy!"

"Run!" yelled Esmeralda.

Trundle ran. A shot rang out, echoing under the archway. There was a sharp crack, and a splinter of stone sliced through Trundle's spines, only just missing his eye.

"Blast you, you cockeyed son of a vole!" hollered Razorback. "Go get 'em, you fools!"

Trundle didn't dare look back as he and Esmeralda raced through the narrow passageways behind Market Square. Above them, the upper floors of the

half-timbered buildings leaned in toward one another, blocking out the sky.

"How far to the docks?" panted Esmeralda.

"Not far now," Trundle gasped, horribly aware of the pounding of following feet and the raucous uproar of pirate voices getting closer by the moment.

He made a skidding turn to the left, grabbing Esmeralda's arm and towing her along behind him. They raced on, passing the Slug and Cabbage Tavern, passing Spadge Hopper's Ironmongery, passing Miss Dolly Buckfur's Ladies' Costumiers, passing so many shops and landmarks that Trundle had known all his life.

The street came to an end, and they found themselves looking out over the wide vistas of the Shiverstones docks. Trundle had never before seen such a terrible sight! Many of the tall warehouses were on fire, the flames leaping high into the night, sending clouds of thick black smoke billowing up to blot out the stars. Even some of the jetties were in flames, and the windships and smaller skyboats moored alongside were smoldering and smoking.

Animals were running hither and thither, pursued by gleeful pirates. Trundle even saw a few bodies: townsfolk killed by the wicked pirates even as they tried to run away.

"There's the *Iron Pig*, Grizzletusk's flagship!" said Esmeralda.

The huge pirate ship was moored alongside Tipplers' Quay, its towering hull armored with overlapping sheets of gray iron, its great mast thrusting up into the night, its bloodred sails billowing.

Long gangplanks led from the *Iron Pig* to the quay and, even as Trundle and Esmeralda watched, more pirates were flooding down the wooden boards, while others were already returning, their arms filled with loot and booty.

"'Ware cannon!" yelped Esmeralda, pulling Trundle down onto the cobbles.

The next second, the air was split by
a thunderous report. Fire flashed
red and white from the
side of the pirate ship
as it rocked backward in
its moorings. Trundle
heard a shrill whistling
overhead. A moment later, there was an explosion
behind them and a chunk of the old Cabbagemongers'
Hall came crashing down into the street.

So that was cannon fire! Trundle had read about
it, but he had never expected it to be so dreadful.

"There they are!" shrieked a voice. It was the rat
again, and there were at least a dozen other pirates at
his back.

Esmeralda grabbed Trundle and hauled him to his
feet. Where could they go? There were pirates everywhere,
and no matter which way they turned, they were
confronted by flames or muskets or gleaming cutlasses.

Following behind in Esmeralda's wake, for a few moments Trundle was just glad to be ahead of their pursuers. But then he saw where she was heading.

"No!" he gasped. "It's a dead end!"

In her panic, Esmeralda had made the fatal mistake of running onto one of the jetties, the long wooden structures that jutted out beyond the rim of the island of Shiverstones. Didn't she realize they would be trapped there? With murderous pirates on one side, and an endless, deadly fall on the other.

Being skewered by pirates was bad enough, but Trundle dreaded falling off the edge of the island. No one really knew what happened when a person fell from an island in the Sundered Lands. The stories said that you fell and fell, until the air got so thin you could hardly breathe and it grew so cold that your eyeballs froze in your head. Then, at last, you would drop out into an empty, starry blackness that went on forever and ever.

"Gotcha!" shrieked the rat as he and his companions blocked the landward end of the jetty. "Frogs 'n' toadies, but you'll regret putting us to such pains, my lovelies! Come on, boys, there's merry work ahead!"

Holding hands, Trundle and Esmeralda backed away from the approaching pirates.

"We're done for!" murmured Trundle. "We should surrender and throw ourselves on their mercy."

"They don't *have* any mercy," said Esmeralda. "Keep a brave heart, Trundle! Something will come up."

A terrific boom sounded from Tipplers' Quay. Nearly shocked out of his prickles by the noise, Trundle snapped his head around to see another of those red-and-white flashes from the side of the *Iron Pig*. The cannon had been fired again.

A high-pitched whistling noise seared the air, horribly near, and the cannonball came crashing through the jetty, sending the wooden boards flying up in a thousand splinters.

"What did I tell you?" shouted Esmeralda. "They'll not get us now!"

With a dreadful creaking and cracking, Trundle felt the planks under his feet give way. The cannonball had torn through the jetty from side to side, and the end upon which the two of them were standing was starting to break away.

There was a final groan as the last supports sheered off, and then the jetty fell away from under them, and Esmeralda and Trundle were sent plunging down into the endless darkness.

3
Badger
Blocks

The stars wheeled giddily around Trundle's head as he plunged downward through empty space. He was just wondering whether death from a musket ball or the quick thrust of a pirate sword might be preferable to this long fall into nothingness, when he landed on something soft and yielding that sent him bouncing breathlessly up into the air again.

His momentum failed and he fell again, his arms and legs flailing. Bounce! He went once more. Up and down, three or four times, and all the while he could hear Esmeralda's laughter ringing in his ears. He came to a final halt and looked dizzily around. Esmeralda was at his side, and the two of them were lying spread-eagled in the wide belly of a canvas tarpaulin.

"What did I tell you?" Esmeralda squealed with delight. "I knew something would come up!"

They had landed on an awning that stretched across part of the deck of a windship. Trundle sat up, gazing around in astonishment. He had never expected to see his homeland from such a peculiar angle.

The great stone crag upon which Shiverstones was founded loomed close by, filling half the sky, looking like a mountain turned upside down, huge and awesome and scary. He could see the broken end of the jetty from which they had fallen, while the other jetties of Port Shiverstones stretched above him, too, like black fingers thrusting out into the night. It was very odd to be looking up at the undersides of all the moored windships. Among the wooden hulls, he quickly spotted the rusty ironclad hulk of the *Iron Pig*.

"That was really lucky!" Trundle blew his cheeks out in disbelief. "What were the odds of landing on a windship?"

"Luck, my prickles!" said Esmeralda. "The Fates are looking out for us, that's what it is."

He eyed her. "You're quite mad," he said. "You know that, don't you?"

A grin slipped up one side of her face, and her eyes sparkled in the gloom. "I'm hungry, I know *that*," she said brightly. "Let's see what kind of windship we've landed on. You never know—the captain may be a friendly fellow who will offer us bed and board for our voyage."

"Our voyage to where?" Trundle asked.

"To the land where the first of the Six Crowns is hidden," Esmeralda said.

"And what land might that be?"

Esmeralda laughed. "If I knew that, this wouldn't be much of a quest, would it?" she said merrily. "Honestly, Trundle, I have no idea where the crown might be hidden—but the Badger Blocks know, and they'll lead us to it."

Trundle shook his head, gazing sadly upward. "Poor Shiverstones," he said. "Will they burn everything, do you think?"

"Let's hope not," said Esmeralda, patting him on the shoulder. "But the best thing we can do for your friends and for everyone else in the Sundered Lands is to find the Six Crowns and then to use their power to rid us of Grizzletusk and his pirates once and for all."

Trundle frowned at her. "There you go again, with your nursery stories," he said, growing a little angry now that he was no longer in fear for his life. He folded his arms and gave her a long, hard look.

"Either you tell me what's going on, or . . . or . . ." His voice faded away.

She tilted her head, giving him a questioning look. "Or?" she prompted.

"I don't know," Trundle admitted grumpily. "Just *tell* me!"

"Very well," Esmeralda began. "In case you haven't worked it out for yourself yet, I am a Roamany. In fact, I am the niece of the one and only Millie Rose Thorne, Roamany queen, fortune-teller, diviner, auger, visionary, haruspex, and soothsayer, renowned throughout all the Sundered Lands for her perspicacity and foresight."

"Never heard of her," Trundle commented. "We don't get many Roamanys in Shiverstones."

"Why am I not surprised about that?" Esmeralda retorted breezily. "Anyway, you've heard of her *now*. This all began one fine day while I was practicing with the Badger Blocks in my aunty's caravan."

"You still haven't told me what these Badger Blocks are," said Trundle.

"They are a set of fifteen ancient wooden blocks, each with four pictures carved on them," explained Esmeralda. "They're kept in the Badger Blocks box. They're extremely old, and they're used to make prophecies and to tell fortunes. The blocks are tipped into a black sack, okay? Then the person wanting to make a reading has to take four blocks out of the bag without looking and lay them down side by side on a table. According to which pictures have come up, and which way around they are, the prophecy can be worked out. Do you get it now?"

"Yes, thank you," said Trundle. "I get it now."

"So, anyway," Esmeralda continued, "my readings usually come out backward or inside out or just plain wrong, but there was something about this particular set of four blocks I'd chosen that made my paws tingle and my whiskers twitch. You see, it started by me choosing the Princess in Darkness, reversed—meaning the wrong way up."

"That's your picture, isn't it?" Trundle said.

"Well remembered! And placing it on the table reversed—upside down—means *problems*. Well, the next block came up with the Lamplighter." She looked at him. "That's you."

"Says *you!*"

"The third block showed the Windship in Full Sail," Esmeralda continued. "That means a lot of traveling. And finally I picked the Six Crowns. And even a half-witted otter knows that the Six Crowns refers to the Six Crowns of the Badgers of Power." She looked urgently at him. "Now do you see?"

Trundle sighed and shook his head.

"The Princess in Darkness and the Lamplighter are meant to go together on a windship to find the Crowns of Power," Esmeralda explained very slowly, as if to a half-witted otter.

"I . . . see . . ." said Trundle, deeply unconvinced.

"I showed the reading to Aunty, of course, but she didn't think it was right; she said I'd gotten things mixed up and I'd pulled out a false reading. I believed her at first, but now I'm sure my reading was a true one." She frowned. "It's odd for Aunty to be wrong about stuff like that, but this time she definitely was!"

Trundle looked at her, thinking how easy life would have been had he managed to get his front door closed before she'd jumped on him.

"And what if this windship *doesn't* take us where you think we need to go?" he asked.

"It will," Esmeralda said. "The Fates will make sure of it."

Trundle was about to let her in on his opinion of the Fates when they heard approaching voices. Esmeralda put a warning paw to her mouth and indicated that they should keep quiet and listen.

"Is all windshipshape and bluffton fashion, Mr. Pouncepot?" asked a gruff voice almost directly under the tarpaulin in which they were sitting. "I'd have us well out of here before we get caught up in Grizzletusk's little brannigan and hullabaloo."

"Aye, Cap'n," said a second voice. "The cargo is secure and the wind is set fair. Just give the word and we'll up sails and be on our way."

"You've scoured the ship for stowaways, have you, Mr. Pouncepot?" asked the first voice. "I'll have no freeloaders and flibbertigibbets on my vessel. Just the sniff of 'em, and I'll have 'em over the side as quick as galley slops!"

Esmeralda and Trundle looked anxiously at each other. That didn't sound so good.

"Aye, Cap'n," said Mr. Pouncepot. "All's clear, bilges to crow's nest."

"Right you are, Pouncepot. Tear down this tarpaulin, and let's be on our way!"

Trundle gave Esmeralda a horrified look as a pair of large clawed paws appeared over the edge of the tarpaulin and took a firm grip.

So much for the Fates, Trundle thought, as the canvas was ripped down and they both went tumbling head over heels toward the deck.

Stowaways
in the
Hold

Trundle plunged headfirst into a barrel half full of hard, lumpy objects, while Esmeralda came thumping down in a tangled heap at his side. He clamped both paws over his mouth to stop himself from yelling with the pain of his landing. Judging from the fading voices of Mr. Pouncepot and the Cap'n, the two of them hadn't been spotted as the awning had been pulled down. Maybe Esmeralda's Fates really were on their side?

Trundle twisted himself around and sat up. The barrel was full of a strong, sweet smell. He reached under himself and pulled out an apple.

"Ouch!" he said softly, rubbing himself here and there. "That hurt!"

"Cheer up," said Esmeralda. "It could have been worse; we might have ended up in a barrel of salted pilchards or pickled eggs."

"We'll be in enough of a pickle if they find us," Trundle said. "You heard what they said: any stowaways will be pitched over the side."

"Then maybe we shouldn't get caught," Esmeralda commented. "From what we heard, this must be a cargo windship. I'd say our best hope of keeping out of sight would be to go down to the hold."

"Whatever you say." Trundle realized she probably had a better idea of how to deal with adventures than he did. He got up and reached for the rim of the barrel.

"Not yet!" said Esmeralda, pulling him back down. "There'll be sailors all over the place while the ship gets going. We'll wait till it's well under way."

They sat together on the lumpy bed of apples, listening to the creak of timbers and the whistle of the wind in the rigging as the sails were set.

The voices of the sailors rang out in a merry chantey as they worked.

We pawned our boots in Widdershins Town—
Go down, ye frogs and toadies!
We'll sail them wild winds round and round—
Yo-ho, ye frogs and toadies!
Go down, ye frogs and toadies-o,
Go down, ye frogs and toads!

We'll haul the mainsail firm and tight—
Go down, ye frogs and toadies!
And set a course by Stonewrack's light—

Yo-ho, ye frogs and toadies!

Go down, ye frogs and toadies-o,

Go down, ye frogs and toads!

The ale is warm, the hammocks cold—

Go down, ye frogs and toadies!

We'll drink and sleep like sailors bold—

Yo-ho, ye frogs and toadies!

Go down, ye frogs and toadies-o,

Go down, ye frogs and toads!

"I like that," murmured Trundle. "I've never heard it before." He sang softly to himself. "Go down, ye frogs and toads." Then he noticed the expression on Esmeralda's face. "What's wrong?" he asked uneasily.

"That's a pirate song," she hissed.

Trundle suddenly felt sick. "You mean we're on a *pirate* windship?"

"I'm not sure. Wait." Esmeralda got to her feet and gradually raised her eyes to the rim of the barrel. She stood there for a few moments before sitting down again.

"No," she said. "They're not pirates, but they look a scurvy, disreputable bunch. The kind that would cut your throat and sell your head as a doorstop." She looked gravely at him. "We are going to have to be very careful, Trundle. Very careful indeed."

Trundle curled himself up among the apples, his chin on his knees and his heart in his mouth. He hardly dared breathe as he listened to the cutthroat sailors going about their noisy and boisterous business. Every now and then, Esmeralda would pop her snout over the rim of the barrel to check out the situation.

Eventually the singing and the hauling and the winching and the stomping about died down.

"Come on," Esmeralda said, giving him a friendly poke. "Here's our chance. Be sharp, now!" She grinned a wild and toothy grin. "And be prepared to fight for your life if they spot us."

Trundle uncurled with a heartfelt groan.

"Only kidding," she said. "We'll be fine."

They slipped over the top of the barrel and jumped down onto the deck. It was a deep, dark starry night and the ship was full of shadows. Trundle spotted a few sailors busy at work, coiling ropes and stowing spare canvas or taking readings from the stars with curious brass instruments. But they were all intent on their jobs and didn't notice the two little animals as they crept through the darkness toward a nearby hatch.

Peering around, Esmeralda lifted the side of the hatch. "Jump," she urged in a soft voice.

Trundle stared down into the darkness. "Are you kidding?" he whispered. "I could break my—"

The rest of the sentence was cut short by Esmeralda grabbing his collar and diving headfirst over the edge of the hatch, dragging him along with her down into the pitch-black hold.

Fortunately they landed on something reasonably soft.

"Well?" chuckled Esmeralda. "*Did* you break anything?"

"I don't know," grumbled Trundle. "It's too dark to tell." He sat up, feeling some kind of cloth under him. "Well, aren't you the clever one," he said with heavy irony. "Here we are in total darkness. I don't suppose it occurred to you that we won't be able to see a single thing down here. Of all the daft—*ohh*!"

A small lemon-colored light had begun to form in the darkness in front of his snout. As the light blossomed, Trundle saw that it was sitting right in the center of Esmeralda's outstretched palm.

"How do you do that?" he asked in an awed voice.

Esmeralda's face appeared, smiling mysteriously beyond the yellowy glow. "I'm a Roamany," she said. "We *know* stuff."

"Do something else!" breathed Trundle. He had always loved the idea of magic, and he had never seen anything so beautiful and strange as Esmeralda's palm light.

"Later, perhaps," she said. "This isn't easy, you know. I have to concentrate really hard."

As the light grew, Trundle saw that they were sitting on top of a pile of cloth bales in a large hold jam-packed with all kinds of goods, supplies, and equipment.

"Interesting," said Esmeralda as they clambered down. "A lot of this looks like mining gear. See those shovels, picks and pitprops, timbers and barrels?"

"Pity there's no food," mused Trundle, his rumbling stomach reminding him that he had not eaten for some time. "I'm quite peckish."

"I'll find us something to eat and drink later," said Esmeralda. "For the moment, let's just make ourselves as comfortable as we can."

They found a pleasant-enough nest for themselves, hidden away among the big black barrels. Trundle listened to the creak and crack of the windship's timbers as it sailed on through the night, taking them who knew where.

"You still haven't told me why the pirates were after you," he said to Esmeralda.

"Well, the very next day after that Badger Block reading I told you about, our convoy was attacked by pirates!" she replied dramatically. "And not just any old pirates: Captain Grizzletusk himself! They took us completely by surprise, whizzing in through the windows and doors of our caravans on long ropes with cutlasses and daggers in their teeth. It was very scary, I can tell you. I grabbed a coal scuttle, ready to whack any pirate who dared to come near. But some sneaky, sly, cowardly, underhanded son of a bilge rat came up behind me, popped a sack over my head, and that was that!"

"Good heavens," murmured Trundle. "You were kidnapped!"

"I was," Esmeralda said, with a hint of pride in her voice. "And they sailed off with me and all the booty aboard the *Iron Pig* and sold me in the slave markets of Drune."

"What's Drune?" asked Trundle.

"Only the most grim and grisly place in the whole of the Sundered Lands," Esmeralda declared. "But not all the guards and chains and locks and bolts in creation could keep me a prisoner!" Her eyes glittered in the yellow light. "I escaped from the mines, slipped aboard the first merchant vessel out of there, and then hopped windship at their first port of call—which just so happened to be Port Shiverstones. And because the Fates were guiding me, that was exactly the place I needed to be. I saw you ambling along and thought, Aha! The Lamplighter! The very fellow I need. So I followed you, and the rest you know."

Trundle nodded thoughtfully, trying to take it all in. It was hard to imagine why the Fates should have picked *him* to help Esmeralda with her escapades. The only adventures he knew about came between the pages of books. And the really good thing about books was that when you were tired or hungry or a bit too scared, you could close them and go and do something else. *Real* adventures, he now realized, weren't quite like that. You couldn't switch them off.

Esmeralda looked quizzically at him. "This is the point where you gasp in amazement and tell me how brave and resourceful I am," she prompted him.

"I'm thirsty," sighed Trundle. "And tired. And hungry."

Esmeralda gave him a friendly pat on the shoulder. "All right," she said gently. "I know this must be hard for you. I'll go get us some food. You stay put."

She muttered something to herself, and the bright little palm light split into two. "Hold out your paw," she said.

Trundle did so, and Esmeralda placed one of the lights on his upturned palm. It felt warm and somehow alive against his skin. He gazed at it, smiling. What a thing! By the time he looked up, meaning to ask Esmeralda about her magic powers, he saw that she had quietly slipped away.

Trundle sighed to himself in the drafty hold, thinking about his comfortable parlor and the winding stairs that led to his cozy bedroom. Who would be there to snuff out the lamps of Port Shiverstones in the morning? Would his friends and

neighbors take to the streets in search
of him? He imagined their anxious
voices, calling out, "Where's
Trundle? What's happened
to good old
reliable Trundle?
We must find him!"

On the other hand, with half the town burned down by
pirates, they might have other things on their minds.

Time passed. He sighed again, idly pulling at a
cork bung that protruded from a hole near the bottom
of the barrel against which he was leaning.

"Oops!" he squeaked as the cork came loose and a
fine dark powder began to pour from the barrel.

"Get away from that stuff!" hissed a voice from
the darkness.

Startled, Trundle got to his feet. "Esmeralda?"

"Don't panic," came her voice. "Just put the
bung back in the barrel and step away over here. And

don't get the palm light anywhere near that powder, or they'll be scraping bits of idiotic hedgehog off the walls for the next ten days!"

Puzzled and alarmed by the tremor in Esmeralda's voice, Trundle jammed the cork in the barrel and backed away.

"I can't leave you alone for five minutes, can I?" said Esmeralda, slapping down on his hand to douse the ball of light. "Don't you know what that stuff is?"

"Not a clue," admitted Trundle, looking ruefully at the small yellowish stain that was left on his palm. "Why? What is it?"

"Only the most dangerous substance to be found anywhere in the Sundered Lands," said Esmeralda. "It's blackpowder!"

"Ohh!" Even Trundle had heard of the terrible blasting powder of the pirates. They used it in their muskets and cannon, and they kept its formula a deadly secret. But one thing Trundle did know was that if you put a flame or anything hot near blackpowder it would go *BOOM!*

He shivered, trying not to think about what would have happened if he had brought the palm light too close, but cheered up a little when he saw that Esmeralda had managed to secure some cheese, bread, and apples, and a flask of water.

They found somewhere to sit as far from the deadly barrels as possible, and ate a reasonably

comforting meal. Then they curled up back-to-back and slept for a while.

❦ ❦ ❦

Trundle was woken by Esmeralda shaking him.

"Wakey, wakey," she hissed in his ear. "We've arrived!"

He sat up, rubbing his eyes and feeling stiff and cold from sleeping on hard windship's boards. "Where?"

"Journey's end!" Esmeralda said excitedly. "Let's go look!"

They managed to find a ladder that took them up to a small hatch with a grate over the top. Esmeralda went first, ducking back under cover every now and then as a burly mariner went stamping past on his way to his post.

At last, they climbed stealthily up onto the main deck. They crept alongside the rail and slipped unobserved into a canvas-covered lifeboat. Hiding under the tarpaulin, Trundle listened to Mr. Pouncepot barking orders, and to the sound of capstans turning and sails being reefed. Esmeralda lifted the edge of the tarpaulin, and he sidled up beside her, peering through the gap.

A knobbly, lumpy, rugged, ugly chunk of rock filled half the sky ahead of them. It wasn't flat topped like Shiverstones, more of a big black ball eaten full of holes and hollows and cavities and craters and caverns.

"Oh, no!" groaned Esmeralda. "Of all the places!"

"What's wrong?" asked Trundle. "Where are we?"

Her voice sounded flat and miserable. "We're right back where I started," she moaned. "This stupid windship has brought me back to Drune!"

RATHANGER

Esmeralda slumped despondently in the bottom of the lifeboat, muttering rude things about the Fates under her breath.

Trundle looked on uneasily and gave her a cautious pat on the shoulder. "There, there," he said. "It'll be all right."

"No, it won't," said Esmeralda. "Everything is wrong, wrong, *wrong*! I knew the cargo was for mine workings, but I didn't know it would be *these* mines!"

I thought it was heading for the steam moles way out in Hammerland."

Trundle peered out from under the tarpaulin. The dismal lump of Drune was looming larger and larger. He couldn't see any sky at all now, and the windship was steering toward a huge round-mouthed chasm. He narrowed his eyes. Yellowy lights were glimmering all around the entrance to the cavern. Lots of lights. Scores of lights. Hundreds of them, in fact.

He let out a low gasp as the windship sailed closer. A town—a tumbledown, ramshackle shantytown— clung around the vast aperture like some kind of horrible fungus. The dilapidated buildings grew out of the rock face, one hovel atop another, the buildings crushed together, misshapen and constricted, as though struggling for space. All of them were shabbily constructed from rotten timbers and crumbling stonework and ill-laid bricks.

Jetties jutted outward, and as the windship glided

into the vast cavern, Trundle could see the shapes of animals scuttling through the shadowy, narrow streets, shoulders hunched, heads down, as though they were engaged on evil errands.

"Welcome to Rathanger," said a mournful voice at Trundle's shoulder. "The last place I ever wanted to see again."

He looked at Esmeralda. "If the Fates are working for us, then perhaps we were *meant* to come here," he said. He wasn't at all sure he believed this, but he wanted very much to cheer her up. If Esmeralda gave up hope, where did that leave him?

She looked at him for a few moments. "You're mostly not as silly as you look," she said at last. "And you're quite right; I should trust the Fates. The Badger Blocks don't lie. We must be here for a reason."

They hove close to a rickety-looking jetty bending under the weight of great piles of boxes and crates and sacks and barrels waiting to be transported to

the black wharves. As the windship came to a gradual
halt, voices called out and ropes were thrown. Dock
rats grabbed the ropes and tied them to rusty iron
bollards. A gangplank was let down.

A pompous-looking muskrat in a long coat
covered in gold braid and gleaming buttons walked
slowly up the gangplank.

"That's the harbormaster," Esmeralda told
Trundle. "Every ship that comes through the town of
Rathanger has to register with him before it's allowed
to sail on into the mine workings." She poked her
head right out to take a better look around. "This is
our chance to get away."

She picked up a length of rope that was coiled
in the bottom of the lifeboat, and Trundle watched
as she tied the end of the rope to a cleat on the
side of the boat. "The worm comes out of its hole,
around the rhubarb stalk, and back down the hole
again," she muttered, tugging on the rope. "There!

A perfect bowline, although I say it myself."

She hefted the rest of the rope onto her shoulder and pushed out from under the tarpaulin. Trundle followed her, and the two of them balanced precariously on the windship's rail.

Esmeralda let down the rope behind a tall stack of wooden crates. "I hope you're good at climbing," she said, catching the rope between her feet and gripping it with her paws as she edged over the windship's side.

"So do I." Trundle didn't bother telling her that he had never climbed a rope before. If he lost his grip, she'd be the first person to know about it.

His stomach turned several somersaults as he hung grimly on to the rope. But it was thick and solid and he had strong paws, and before he knew it, the two of them were down on the jetty, dashing from cover to cover as they made their stealthy way through the wharves and into the cramped and winding streets of Rathanger.

Trundle had never dreamed of such an awful place. Not only were the buildings crushed so close together that the roofs often overlapped one another across the streets, but the whole town stank horribly. The switchback streets and alleys were piled with rubbish and filled with disreputable-looking creatures, dressed shabbily and carrying swords or knives or cudgels.

"Avoid eye contact," Esmeralda warned him. "Keep your head down and keep moving—and try not to look like an easy target. This place is full of gambling dens and drinking houses and other much nastier places that you'd rather not know about. Treat everyone you meet as a potential thief, and you won't go far wrong."

"So where exactly are we going?" asked Trundle.

"We're following our noses. The Fates will do the rest!"

Trundle wasn't so much following his nose as holding it to keep out the unpleasant odors. They slipped through an alley. The sound of a badly tuned piano rang out from an open doorway, accompanied by a fume of pipe smoke and the foul smell of stale beer. Drunken voices caterwauled an incoherent ditty about knives and murder, with the refrain:

Blood, blood, buckets of blood,
Nothing quite like it for thick'ning the mud!

Trundle looked up at the hanging inn sign.

THE STRANGLED STOAT
PROPRIETOR: PUNCHLY BACKBREAKER
LICENSED TO SELL HARD LIQUOR.
GAMBLING ACTIVELY ENCOURAGED.
COME ON IN AND LOSE YOUR LITTLE ALL!

He thought of the kind and hospitable folk of Port Shiverstones and shuddered quietly to himself.

From the street ahead, there came the sound of voices shouting and of whips cracking and chains clanking. Esmeralda grabbed Trundle and pulled him into a shadowy doorway. "Shhh! Slave traders!" she hissed.

A few moments later, Trundle saw a long, chained line of miserable-looking animals being herded along by a bunch of burly rats wielding whips.

"Keep moving, you scum!" bellowed the lead rat. "There might be rumblings of rebellion from the mines, but there'll be no mutinies among my band of merry volunteers!" A whip cracked, followed by cries and groans.

Trundle watched in mute horror as the line of wretched captives stumbled past the end of the alley. He looked at Esmeralda. Her teeth were gritted, and her eyes glittered with anger.

"They treated *me* like that a few days ago," she muttered.

"Can we help them?" asked Trundle.

"We can't free them, if that's what you mean," she replied. "We'll do our bit by following our quest. Perhaps when the Six Crowns of the Badgers are reunited, horrid places like this will cease to exist."

The sounds of the slave line faded away into the general discord of the town.

Trundle shook his head, wishing he were a real hero, a creature brave and strong and noble enough to help those poor prisoners.

"Something like *that* would probably be useful," he said, pointing toward a dingy, dusty, murky window on the other side of the alley, through which the outline of a sword could dimly be seen. "Not that I'd know how to use it."

Three brass balls hung above the shop door, and there was a dirty sign over it that read:

Honesty Skank's
Gold Star Pawnshop
We Buy Anything from Anyone
Step Inside and Do a Deal

"Oh, well," he said. "No good wishing for things we can't have." He turned and walked along the alley, assuming Esmeralda would come with him.

She didn't. She stood as stiff and still as a startled starfish, staring round-eyed through the window of the pawnshop.

Trundle waited a few moments, then walked back to where she was standing.

"What are you looking at?" he asked.

"The sword!" she said, in a trembling, choking voice. "Look at the sword!"

He stepped up close to the window and looked. The sword was clearly old; it had notches in the blade and looked in need of a good polish.

"Yes?" he said. "So?"

Esmeralda whipped out the Badger Block and brandished it in front of his snout, showing him the Lamplighter picture. "See?" she said, with hardly contained excitement. "It's exactly the same!"

Trundle looked from the real sword to the picture of the sword in the carved Lamplighter's hand. "They are quite similar," he admitted.

"Similar?" Esmeralda raged. "They're the same in

every detail. That's why the Fates brought us here—
to get this sword! It all makes sense now!"

Trundle brought his snout up to the dirty glass.
"It has a price tag on the handle," he said. "Twenty
sunders." He frowned. "That's quite a lot of money.
I don't have a single sunder on me. How about you?"

Esmeralda shook her head, but Trundle could see
her mind was working.

"We need to get money fast," she said. "Tell you
what—let's find a quiet, out-of-the-way place. I'll hide
while you go up to the first person who happens along.
Ask him the way to Slitherslops Street, or some such, and
while he's not looking, I'll sneak up behind and whack
him over the head with a brick. Then before he comes
around, we'll swipe his wallet, and hey presto—we buy
the sword." She paused and frowned at him. "You've
got an expression on your face like a warthog chewing
a bumblebee," she said. "What's the problem?"

Trundle hardly knew where to start. "We can't

attack people and steal their money!" he gasped.

Her eyebrows rose. "We can't?"

"No! Not at all. Never. No how! It's just *wrong!*"

Esmeralda shrugged. "Oh, all right, Mr. Scruples," she said, a little sulkily. "If you say so. Come on then, let's hear *your* plan for making money."

"Couldn't we get a job of some sort?" he suggested. "Um . . . cleaning windows, or sweeping the streets, or something like that?"

"Does Rathanger look like the kind of place where they pay people to clean their windows and sweep the streets?" Esmeralda asked. "But still, if you're determined not to go along with my perfectly reasonable plan, I suppose we'll have to come up with *something.*" She narrowed her eyes and tapped at her front teeth with her claws. "Yes!" she said after a few moments. "I think I know what to do." She turned on her heel and strode off, Trundle trotting along to keep up with her. "Mugging is easier, but if you insist on being awkward, we'll probably be able to make some quick money clearing glasses or serving drinks in a pub."

She pointed to the crude illustration of a stoat being throttled that hung above the open door they had recently passed. "In *that* pub, to be exact."

"It looks a little . . . um . . . rough," Trundle pointed out.

"We could go back to plan A," Esmeralda suggested, miming clouting someone with a brick.

"No," Trundle said firmly. "We'll try in there."

They pushed their way into the fuggy, stinky, crowded inn, squeezing between the seedy clientele, heading for the long, stained, and dripping bar.

Esmeralda led Trundle behind the bar, where the floor was awash with spilled ale and the stench was strong enough to fell an ox. She tugged at the apron of a portly rat with a ruddy face, a crooked snout, and a mouthful of broken teeth. "Are you the landlord?" she shouted above the noise.

"What if I am?" boomed the rat.

"We're looking for work," Esmeralda yelled. "Anything will do. Bar work, kitchen work—you name it."

The landlord looked them up and down. "You look too puny," he declared.

"We're stronger than you might think," said Esmeralda. "I work out regularly, and my friend here is the all-in urchin-weight wrestling champion of

Shiverstones." She looked meaningfully at Trundle. "Aren't you?"

Trundle adopted what he hoped looked like an aggressive, muscular pose.

"I certainly am!" he growled.

Punchly Backbreaker roared with laughter. "If you say so," he gurgled. "Get into the kitchens with you, then—there's plenty of dishes needing to be washed. Half a sunder an hour. Take it or leave it."

Esmeralda held out a paw. "One sunder in advance, for good faith," she said.

"Done!" Punchly Backbreaker fished a wet sunder out of his apron pocket and dropped it into her paw.

"Thank you very much, sir," said Trundle. "We won't let you down, I promise."

"All-in wrestling champion!" hooted Punchly, and he howled with laughter again.

They were about to go through the door that led to the kitchens when a loud, grating voice rang out above the noise. "Tap your finest ale, landlord! Bring on the dancing girls! Clear the poker tables! The *Iron Pig* has just made landfall, and Captain Grizzletusk and his crew have a powerful thirst on them!"

"Lawks!" exclaimed Esmeralda, grabbing Trundle and yanking him through the doorway and into the foul-smelling kitchen. Her eyes were filled with unease. "Are they on our trail? Do they know we're here? Are they already lying in wait for us?" She clutched at her neck, as though she could already feel the sting of a jagged blade across her windpipe.

"It's probably just a coincidence," Trundle said hopefully. "So long as we keep out of sight, we should be fine." He looked around the kitchen. It was unspeakably filthy, with thick grease on every surface and squashed food all over the floor. Punchly Backbreaker had not been wrong about the washing up: plates and bowls and cutlery and mugs and cups were stacked almost ceiling high around the low butler's sink.

"It looks as if no one's done any washing up for ten years!" gasped Esmeralda, peering into the scummy water in the sink.

"Which means there's enough work to earn us the money we need," Trundle said, trying to look on the bright side. "And if the pirates come in here, we can nip out the back way." He pointed to the glass-paneled back door, through which outside walls were visible.

"Hmmm," said Esmeralda. She walked gingerly across the slithery floor and pressed her ear to the wooden panels of another door, set in the side wall. "Hmmm," she said again. "Interesting."

"What?" asked Trundle.

"Voices," said Esmeralda. A grin spread across her face, and she spun the landlord's sunder in the air. "You start working," she said, turning the handle and pulling the side door open a crack. "I shan't be long."

"Hey, hold on—"

"Gentlemen," Trundle heard her say as she

slipped through the door and let it swing behind her, "how delightful to meet you! May I join you in your game of chance? I don't have very much experience with poker, but I would love to learn."

The door clicked shut. Trundle glared expressively at the cracked panels for a few moments. Then he turned to the washing up. Drat the girl, he thought, staring up at the teetering towers of filthy crocks. Typical of her to avoid the hard work! Still, there was nothing to be gained by fuming. He rolled up his sleeves and got busy, concentrating on the money that his labors would provide.

It wasn't long before he was sick of the sight of putrid plates and dirty dishes and nasty knives and filthy forks. Every now and then he would glance angrily toward the closed door. What was that dratted Roamany girl doing in there?

Suddenly he became aware of a rumpus coming from beyond the door: furious yelling and the thud of furniture overturning. A split second later, the door sprang open and Esmeralda appeared, looking triumphant but somewhat flustered. She slammed the door and pressed her back against it, panting.

"I've got the money we need," she gasped. "But I think I may have gotten us into a spot of trouble!"

Trundle stared at her in alarm. He could hear creatures shouting and pounding on the door. Clearly, Esmeralda had done something to make them very angry indeed, and the way the door was bulging inward, he guessed it wouldn't be long before they smashed their way through, to take their revenge.

6

THE PERILS OF CHEATING AT CARDS

"What did you *do* in there?" wailed Trundle, as the door reverberated to the thumps and kicks of far too many furious fists and feet.

"No time for explanations!" cried Esmeralda. "Quickly! Hand me a knife!"

Trundle snatched a knife out of the washing-up water and ran over to her. Was she planning on fighting? If so, what should he do? Attack with his dish mop?

She jammed the knife under the door, wedging it shut—for the moment!

"Come on!" she yelled, grabbing Trundle's hand and towing him to the back door. "We need to skedaddle!" She waved a bunch of paper sunders at him. "We can afford the sword now!"

They plunged through the back door and found themselves in a dimly lit back alley.

"How did you get the money?" gasped Trundle as they ran over cobbles.

"I won it fair and square at poker," Esmeralda explained breathlessly. "But they caught me cheating, curse them for suspicious swine!" She laughed. "They'll never find us now, Trundle, my lad! We're home free!"

At that moment, the back door of the kitchen burst open and a gang of disreputable-looking rats came pouring out into the alley.

"There she is!" screamed one of them, pointing a

claw. "Get her, boys! We'll show her how we deal with card sharps in this town!"

"Oh, lummy!" gasped Esmeralda. "Run, Trundle! Run!"

But Trundle didn't need telling. He was already running.

They dived around a zigzag bend, pursued by the yelling mob of irate gamblers. Trundle quickly lost all sense of direction as they raced up and down and to and fro and hither and thither through the winding, twisting, turning tangle of passageways and lanes and alleys of Rathanger. And always, their pursuers were only half a street away from them, wielding sticks and cudgels and bludgeons, and yelling terrible threats.

At one point, Esmeralda paused for a moment to pick up a loose cobblestone. For a horrible moment, Trundle thought she was going to stand and fight the rats, but she just carried on running, her skirts flying.

Suddenly Trundle realized where they were. Their mad chase had brought them right back to where they had started—in the same alley as the entrance to the Strangled Stoat. Esmeralda came to a skidding halt, leaning back and hefting the cobblestone. She let it fly. There was a chime and clash of smashing glass, and almost before Trundle knew what was going on, she had reached in through the broken window of Honesty Skank's Gold Star Pawnshop and had grabbed hold of the sword.

A shrill alarm bell began to clang from inside the shop.

Esmeralda pushed the sword into Trundle's hands. "Yours, I think," she panted. "I should have thought of this from the start! It would have saved us a lot of bother!"

"But we can't—"

A ferocious ferret appeared at the shop door, armed with an ax. "Gertcha, you spiny stealers!" he

snarled. "I'll have your paws for earmuffs!"

At the same moment the mob of angry gamblers came scooting around the corner.

"Aha!" they cried.

"Oho!" growled Honesty Skank, stepping into the alley with his ax held high.

"Leg it!" yelled Esmeralda.

Clutching the sword to his chest with both arms, Trundle legged it.

Should I stand and fight now that I'm armed? he asked himself as he hurtled along at Esmeralda's side. Not unless I want to be beaten to a pulp and then carved up into mincemeat, he advised himself.

It was a compelling argument.

He carried on running.

They were footing it at top speed along a particularly skinny alleyway that ran between tall brick walls studded with doors. One door hung partly open on a single hinge. Esmeralda zipped through,

Trundle right behind her. They found themselves in some kind of backyard, filled with all manner of debris.

"Block the door!" gasped Esmeralda. Trundle slipped the sword into his belt and, working furiously alongside Esmeralda, helped heap against the doorway every piece of rubble he could lay his paws on.

"They went through here!" shouted a voice from the alley.

"Let's go!" said Trundle.

Hand in hand, they scrambled over the rubbish in the yard to the foot of a rusty iron spiral staircase. Up they went, like a pair of squirrels in a tree, racing round and round till Trundle was dizzy. Just as he was about to fall over, they came to a balcony with an open doorway and stumbled inside.

"Hey! Who are you?" demanded a huge female rat, standing at a bubbling cauldron and stirring the contents with a big ladle. All around her, child rats were clamoring and yowling and holding up food bowls.

"Hovel inspectors, ma'am," said Esmeralda. "Don't panic, we're just passing through."

They waded through the braying rat brats, trying to avoid being bitten and clawed and hit with bowls while the mother yelled and swung at them with her ladle.

Trundle came to an inner doorway, Esmeralda just one pace behind. "Nice hovel!" she called back. "Enjoy your slops."

The ladle whizzed past her ear as Trundle hauled her into the corridor. Behind them, they heard a renewed hubbub from the rat kitchen, accompanied by yelps as the pursuing gamblers encountered Mrs. Rat and her hungry family.

Trundle pushed open the nearest door. A large, stout, elderly rat was standing stark naked in a tub of steaming water, attacking his hard-to-reach parts with a foaming scrub brush.

"Oops! Beg pardon!" said Trundle, backing out and slamming the door.

They carried on down the corridor. Trundle could hear Esmeralda giggling, and soon he was laughing as well.

"I didn't even know rats took baths," she gurgled.

"By the look of him, they don't very often," chuckled Trundle.

The next doorway took them out into the open again. They ran across a curving wooden bridge, horribly aware of its boards creaking and cracking under them. There was a platform at the far end of the bridge, offering several options: stairways and doorways and even a ladder that led to a hatchway up above.

"Stop! Thieves!"

They stared back. Their angry pursuers were at the other side of the bridge, wielding their clubs and cudgels.

"Up!" said Esmeralda.

"The ladder doesn't look very safe," Trundle worried.

"Exactly!"

She swarmed up the ladder. Trundle took one look at the angry mob about to cross the bridge and decided to risk it.

The ladder swayed and wobbled alarmingly as the two animals ascended. The climb was made even more tricky for Trundle because the point of his sword kept getting caught between the rungs. He had half a mind to pull the awkward thing out of his belt and let it drop, except that he couldn't spare a paw to do so. Besides, he knew Esmeralda would probably throw *him* down the ladder if he arrived at the top without the precious sword.

With a scramble and a scrabble and a nasty moment when the handle of the sword got wedged, Trundle eventually hauled himself up through the trapdoor, to emerge in a storeroom heaped with sacks of flour.

"Can't . . . run . . . much . . . farther. . . ." he gasped, tottering to his feet, his legs feeling very feeble under him. "Maybe we could slow them down by pelting them with flour sacks?"

"Possibly," said Esmeralda, kneeling on the floor and leaning out over the hatchway. "Or maybe we could do *this*!" She grabbed hold of the top of the ladder and tried to twist it. "Help me out here, Trundle!"

He got down beside her. The first few gamblers had already started climbing the ladder, were on their way up, and looked pretty murderous.

Trundle added his paws to Esmeralda's on the ladder, and they both hauled at it.

"Hoy!" came an alarmed cry from below. "Don't do that!"

"Good-bye, boys, it was nice knowing you," Esmeralda called down as the two of them gave the ladder a final hefty wrench. Suddenly it spun out of their paws. It teetered for a few moments, standing unsupported in the air with five yelling rats clinging to it. Then, quite slowly at first, it began to tip over backward.

Esmeralda stood up and slammed the hatch shut on the howling and crashing from below. "Nice work!" she said, smacking her paws together. "Let's get out of here."

"I hope they weren't hurt too badly," said Trundle, as he followed her out of the storeroom.

"I hope they *were*," said Esmeralda.

"But they were only chasing us because you cheated them," Trundle pointed out.

Esmeralda turned and placed a paw on each of his shoulders. "Trundle, you have to get your priorities right," she said. "Are we on an important quest, or are we not?"

"I suppose we are," Trundle admitted. "Sort of."

"Sort of!" exploded Esmeralda. "Did we miraculously escape the pirates in Shiverstones, or not? Did the windship bring us here, or didn't it? Do we have the Lamplighter's sword, or don't we?"

"We did, it did, and we have," agreed Trundle. "But I'm not entirely comfortable with a quest that involves cheating and stealing and chucking people off ladders, that's all."

Esmeralda smiled indulgently at him. "Would you rather we didn't have the sword and those ruffians had caught us?" she asked.

"Well, no . . ."

"Attaboy!" she said. "Come on, we've got what we came here for. Let's find our way back to the docks and jump a windship off this devilish lump of rock!"

They walked along the streets of Rathanger, Esmeralda's arm tucked into Trundle's as they made their way back to the jetties and wharves. It was nice not to be chased, and to be on the safe side, they were keeping as much as possible to the less crowded thoroughfares, just in case Honesty Skank was on the prowl, wanting his sword back.

Trundle sauntered along with one paw resting on the hilt of his newfound weapon. He had no idea how to use the thing, but it felt rather impressive to have it tucked into his belt.

Esmeralda seemed in high spirits. "That was quite the adventure, wasn't it?" she said. "And now that we have the Lamplighter's sword, nothing in all the Sundered Lands can stop us!"

"Is that so, my pretty?" growled a deep, throaty voice from the shadow of an archway that stood just ahead of them. "I beg to differ, little ones! I beg to differ!"

A harsh, shrill voice croaked. "Beg to differ! Beg to differ!"

From the deep shade stepped a huge scarred hog with a long purple feather in his hat and a wicked-looking raven perched on his shoulder.

"Razorback!" groaned Esmeralda. "Of all the rotten luck!"

Unwittingly they had stumbled right into the path of Captain Grizzletusk's dreadful bosun. From the evil look in his eye, he wasn't about to let them escape his clutches!

RAZORBACK AND THE RAVEN

"There's a nice fat bounty on your head, little girl," growled Razorback, grinning hideously. "The mine rats give a hundred sunders for every captured runaway."

"Is that dead or alive?" Esmeralda asked. In the circumstances, Trundle was impressed by the steadiness of her voice.

"Either works for me," said Razorback.

"Dead or alive!" croaked Captain Slaughter. "Dead or alive!"

A kind of reckless courage overtook Trundle. He was so certain he would be spending the rest of his life chained up in a mine, he found he didn't really care about anything anymore.

"Oh, shut up, bugle beak!" he shouted at the raven. "I've never seen anyone so ugly in my entire life! Is that your own face, or are you wearing it for a bet?"

The raven ruffled its feathers and leaned down toward him, fixing him with a penetrating eye. "Watch it, matey!"

"Way to go, Trundle!" breathed Esmeralda, her eyes shining with a new admiration. She looked up at Razorback. "I've got fifty paper sunders here," she said, showing him the wedge of money. "You get it if you let the kid go. I hardly even know him, and he's not worth a bean to you."

"Hey!" cried Trundle. "I'm not a kid! And I'm not abandoning you, either!"

"Shhh!" hissed Esmeralda. "It's for your own good."

Razorback laughed. "I get the money either way, girlie," he said. "And your pal there will sell for a few sunders in the slave market, I don't doubt. Now then, are you going to come quietly, or do I need to get the iron muzzles out?"

Trundle leaped in front of Esmeralda. "Touch one prickle on her head, and you'll have me to answer to!" he shouted, trying desperately to pull the sword out of his belt. But its hilt had somehow become caught up in his clothes, and it wouldn't budge. As he struggled, he had the feeling that the delay had rather taken the edge off his courageous act. That, and the fact that Razorback and Captain Slaughter were rocking with laughter.

"Shut your beak, you mangy sparrow!" Trundle yelled at the cackling raven. "Just you wait! I'll trim your tail feathers for you! I'll pluck you raw and truss you up and pop you in the oven to roast, you puffed-up piece of paltry, pop-eyed poultry!" Trundle couldn't imagine where all these words were coming from. It wasn't like him at all.

Trundle's abuse was too much for Captain Slaughter. With a wrathful croak that sounded like fingernails scraping down a blackboard, he launched himself off the bosun's shoulder, his wings outstretched, his wicked sharp beak aiming for Trundle's face.

"Watch out!" screamed Esmeralda.

Trundle made a half turn, intending to dive out of the way, but at that moment, the sword came free and his arm jerked back and his elbow accidentally went *smack*, right into the raven's eye.

"Arrghawkkkk!" With a croak of shock and pain, the raven crashed to the cobbles in a wild tangle of beak and claws and feathers.

"Hah!" yelled Trundle, waving his sword in the air. "Take that!"

"I'll take it, all right," thundered Razorback. "I'll take it and chop you into collops with it!"

He loomed over Trundle, claws poised to snatch. But then from behind Trundle, a cobblestone came whizzing through the air, launched by Esmeralda. It hit Razorback right on the snout. The bosun went cross-eyed with agony and staggered about, clutching his wounded nose with both paws and howling while Trundle danced with joy, swiping at him with the sword.

There was a fearful squawk as Razorback accidentally trod on Captain Slaughter, followed by a yowl of pain from the bosun as the squashed bird reverted to instinct and stabbed him in the foot with its beak.

"Escaping now would be good," said Esmeralda, snatching at Trundle's jacket.

They sped away.

"We beat them!" gasped Trundle. "Did you hear me? Did you hear the things I was saying?"

"Yes," panted Esmeralda. "I was impressed."

"We beat the worst pirate in the world!" yelled Trundle, swinging his sword as he ran.

"The *second* worst pirate in the world," Esmeralda corrected him. "You haven't met Captain Grizzletusk yet."

"All the same!" Trundle was almost dizzy with triumph. "I've never had so much fun in my life. We should go back and finish them off!"

"Get a grip!" said Esmeralda. "We were lucky. Don't count on it happening again. We need to get far, far away from here! If they catch us, they'll kill us in a very special and very slow piratey way. Trust me!"

There was an angry roar from behind them. Trundle glanced over his shoulder, and his brief joy evaporated. Razorback was pounding along the alley in high rage, and at the speed he was moving, he'd be within claw's reach in no time.

The two hedgehogs skedaddled down the alley at top speed, all thoughts of returning to finish off the evil bosun quite forgotten by Trundle in his panic to escape.

❧ ❧ ❧

Trundle and Esmeralda fled deeper into the vast dark chasm of Drune. They had left the flickering lights of Rathanger behind and were running hand in hand up a steep black slope of slippery, slithery, shiny rock. Below them, a road wound on into the chasm, lit by the bloodred flames of iron braziers. At the far end of this road, Trundle could dimly see a cluster of similar ruddy lights.

"Those are the mines," Esmeralda explained as they sat for a moment on a flat chunk of rock perched above the road, catching their breath.

"We don't want to go there, surely?" panted Trundle.

"Of course not," said Esmeralda. "The plan is to sit tight up here till Razorback goes past, then double back and make for the docks." She peered along the road as it wound into Rathanger. "He was right behind us all the way," she said in a puzzled voice. "Where's he gone? He won't have given up. What's he playing at?"

"I don't know and I don't care," said Trundle,

leaning back against a shard of rock. "But I'll tell you something for nothing: I'm getting really tired of being chased all the time."

"A few minutes ago you were telling me how much fun you were having," Esmeralda pointed out. "Some people are very fickle."

Trundle gave her a long-suffering look but said nothing.

Esmeralda sat staring back down the road. "Odd," she murmured to herself. "Very odd."

"I think he's given up," Trundle said after a little while.

"I wouldn't bet on it. Look!"

Trundle joined Esmeralda at the lip of black rock. A bunch of piratical shapes were moving along the road from Rathanger. At their head was the disturbingly familiar bulk of Razorback. The only comfort Trundle took was that there was no sign of Captain Slaughter. It was too much to hope that the horrible bird had been squashed to death back in Rathanger, but at least the bosun's homicidal sidekick seemed to be too poorly to join in the hunt.

Trundle saw a long leash extending from Razorback's fist. A small scuttling creature was attached to its far end. The little animal ran on ahead of him, skipping back and forth across the width of the road, its long thin snout to the ground.

"What is *that*?" Trundle asked.

"A sniffer shrew," Esmeralda said unhappily. "I hadn't counted on that. Those animals can track a mayfly over moving water!" She dodged out of sight and stood up. "Come on, we're not safe here. That shrew will lead them right to us. We have to move."

They scrambled along the precarious rock face, keeping close together, using both paws and both feet to save themselves from missing their footing on the glassy hillside. The last thing they needed was to go tobogganing down onto the road, right in the path of the hunting pirates and their long-nosed sniffer shrew.

As they made their way forward, Trundle looked back. The shrew had led Razorback and several of the pirates up onto the hillside. The rest were following along the road, cutlasses and long knives at the ready.

He could hear the sniffer shrew's high-pitched, whiny voice in the distance. "This way, boss—they went this way for sure. Follow me, boss. Follow me."

"I'd like to tie that animal's snout in a knot," Trundle growled.

"The only way we're going to get out of this is to hide our scent," said Esmeralda. "If we stay up here, we're pretty much done for." She looked grimly at Trundle. "We have to go into the mines."

He blinked at her. "So, to save ourselves from being caught and forced to go into the mines, we're *going into the mines*. Is that your plan?"

"It is," Esmeralda said. "Remember, I escaped once. I can certainly do it again. Trust me. This is the only way to throw that sniffer shrew off our scent. He won't be able to find us in the crowd."

"Go on, then," sighed Trundle. "I'm right behind you."

They scurried as quickly as possible across the hillside. Now Trundle could hear the screaking sounds of winches and the whirring of flywheels. The pounding of jackhammers made the ground tremble under his feet. Right below them, he could see a cluster of dirty shacks and sheds, and a narrow jetty that thrust out into the darkness of the chasm, lit all along its length by braziers on iron tripods.

Moored at the far end of the jetty was the same windship that had brought them to Drune in the first place. Creatures were moving to and fro, unloading the cargo and hefting it into the sheds. There were also a lot of much smaller skyboats moored higgledy-piggledy along the sides of the jetty, dozens of them—scores of them, in fact—looking to Trundle like almond-shaped leaves growing from a big black tree branch.

"The mine guards use the skyboats to ferry stuff to and fro from Rathanger," Esmeralda explained.

Trundle thought for a moment how nice it would be to jump into one of those leaf-shaped skyboats and sail away home in it. Dismissing his daydream, he followed Esmeralda down from the hillside and in behind the sheds. New sounds came to his ears: the steady rhythm of picks and shovels and club hammers, and the noise of shouting voices and cracking whips and clanking chains.

With Esmeralda in the lead, the two hedgehogs slipped into the mines through a wide cave mouth. The air was foul and full of choking dust. Lanterns were hooked to the walls, but the light they gave off was weak and smoky.

"Move, you filthy maggots!" roared a voice. A dismal metallic grinding noise sounded from deeper in the cave. Esmeralda and Trundle ducked for cover as a wagon came into view, loaded with coal, hauled along iron rails by woeful and suffering animals in leather harnesses, with chains hanging from their wrists and ankles. A warthog cracked a long whip above their heads.

The two of them waited till the wagon had gone past, then crept deeper down the tunnel into the cave—deeper into the dreadful and dangerous mines of Drune.

The Mines of Drune

The tunnel opened out into a huge cavern lit by flickering torches and glowing iron braziers. Trundle was appalled by the abominable sight that met his eyes. The great walls of the cavern stepped up into terrace after miserable terrace; on every level, scores of slaves were hacking at the coal face. More slaves were gathering the coal in baskets and climbing up and down rickety ladders to deposit the foul stuff in iron wagons. The heat was oppressive, and the air was thick with the stench of sweat and coal dust and cruelty and despair.

Trundle shivered with dismay and pity for the poor slave workers. As if their plight wasn't grim enough, warthogs and boars and rats and pigs strode about, shouting constantly and wielding whips and cudgels, laying into them seemingly on a whim.

"This is awful," he breathed.

"Tell me about it," murmured Esmeralda. "I spent two weeks in here before I managed to escape. Come on, let's mingle before that sniffer shrew turns up."

It was all too easy to creep from the shadowy tunnel and make their way in among a bunch of slaves who were carrying baskets to one of the wagons. Hopeless eyes stared at them from blackened faces.

"Hide us, please," said Esmeralda. "We're in trouble with the pirates."

. Wordlessly, the slaves gathered around the two hedgehogs, shielding them from the guards' sight as they plodded along. Esmeralda and Trundle helped heft the coal into the wagon, keeping among the sad animals as they turned and made their way back to the coal face for another load.

"You might be better off with the pirates than ending up here," said an emaciated old hare, shaking his long head. "No one ever gets out of these mines alive."

"I did," said Esmeralda. "And we will again."

"You should come with us!" said Trundle.

The hare lifted his wrists, the rusty chains clanking as they ran from creature to creature. "How?" he asked.

"There must be keys to unlock the chains," Trundle said.

"There are," said the hare. "Overseer Grunther keeps them."

He gestured toward a truly massive female hog, who stood with her feet wide apart and her fists on her hips, staring balefully around the mine with a look in her eyes that made Trundle's spine turn to water. A thick leather belt wound around her expansive waist, and hanging from iron hooks fixed to the belt were an assortment of keys.

Trundle looked into the hare's sorry eyes. "I promise that if we get out, we'll find a way to release you all," he said solemnly.

He saw Esmeralda looking at him with knitted brows, but he didn't care what she thought of his rash pledge. He really meant it: if there was a way to rescue these creatures, then he was determined to try.

They plodded with the slaves up a long slope that led to the first level of the workings. Cracked and broken shards of coal were heaped beside each worker, waiting to be loaded into the baskets and taken away.

"Get down!" hissed Esmeralda, dropping to her knees and pulling Trundle down with her.

"Grunther!" bellowed a familiar voice. "Overseer Grunther, where are you, you old drab!"

Razorback stood in the mouth of the tunnel through which Trundle and Esmeralda had just come.

The sniffer shrew was straining at the leash, running back and forth, sneezing every now and then from the coal dust getting into his snout. Several pirates stood alongside Razorback, grim and mean and murderous.

Overseer Grunther turned and trudged toward the group of pirates.

"Well, bosun?" she asked. "Have you brought back our little runaway?"

Razorback gestured at the sniffer shrew. "Snivel thinks she came this way, with a companion. Another hedgehog, a tubby little creature with an idiotic face and a blunt old sword. You've not seen them?"

Grunther's small eyes glittered. "I have not," she growled. "But if they're here, we'll winkle 'em out, have no fear."

Trundle glared down at the pirate hog. He had half a mind to leap down on Razorback and teach him a lesson! Idiotic face, indeed!

The sniffer shrew hunkered down on its haunches,

its eyes and nose streaming. "I've lost them, boss," it whined, wiping a skinny paw across its nose. "I can't smell nuffin' in here. The coal dust do get up my hooter, so."

A soft voice hissed in Trundle's ear. "You need to get out of here, right now." It was the old hare. "Overseer Grunther will organize a roll call. You'll be found. Go quickly, before she sounds the siren."

Esmeralda and Trundle crawled as fast as they could along the terrace, trying always to keep behind the heaps of fresh-cut coal. They were already a fair distance from Razorback when a terrible, deafening horn blared out.

The echoes of the siren were still bouncing from wall to wall as Overseer Grunther began to shout. "Stop work! Leave your tools where they are. Make your way off the terraces and assemble in ranks. Guards, look out for two hedgehogs without chains. Sharp, now!"

Whips cracked, and the slaves began to shuffle toward the ladders.

"Hello, my beauties," snarled a grinning warthog, standing suddenly over Trundle and Esmeralda with a whip poised. "And where might you be going, without your chains and all?"

"Wouldn't you like to know!" In the blink of an eye, Esmeralda dived forward, her spiky head connecting hard with the warthog's stomach. He stumbled backward with a grunt of pain, and the next second he went toppling off the terrace, hitting the ground with a loud crash.

The noise of the warthog's fall did not go unnoticed.

"Get 'em!" howled Overseer Grunther, pointing a podgy paw.

"Snatch them!" bellowed Razorback. "Catch them, crush them, squish them, squash them! Five hundred sunders for the animal who takes them alive!"

Trundle and Esmeralda ran for it, the slaves stepping back to allow them past as they pelted along the terrace.

There was a cave! A tunnel! An even blacker mouth in the wall of black coal! They threw themselves into it, racing over the uneven floor while the tunnel swallowed them like a long dark throat.

"Ouch!" gasped Trundle, running blindly into an invisible rock face. "Esmeralda! I can't see a thing."

A soft pop sounded close by, and a small, round, lemon-colored light appeared, illuminating Esmeralda's face and paw. By the soft glow of the palm light they saw the tunnel turn a corner, veering off at odd angles as it burrowed into the rock. They ran, side by side, panting as the hot, dusty air choked their noses and clogged their windpipes.

Trundle's chest was hurting, and he didn't think he could go on much farther, but a loud noise from far too close behind helped change his mind. Several pairs of heavy boots were thumping along the tunnel. Now the tunnel forked; making an instant choice, they raced down the left-hand shaft. A few moments later Trundle heard Razorback's voice.

"Abigail Frutch, Willie Stiggle, Hacksaw Scarsnout, follow me. The rest of you, go the other way! Don't kill 'em—we're going to have some fun with 'em first!"

Trundle didn't like the sound of that. A pirate's idea of fun wasn't something he liked to think too much about—especially as he and Esmeralda were to be on the receiving end.

They ran on, guided by the gentle radiance of Esmeralda's palm light, bobbing and weaving this way and that as the path switched directions. It was an odd tunnel. It didn't seem to know which way it wanted to go; up, down, to the left, to the right, making sudden hairpin turns and corkscrew twists for no apparent reason.

"I'm beginning to think a drunken badger must have dug this out," Trundle panted.

"It's part of the old silver mines," gasped Esmeralda. "Before the miners ever bothered with the coal, they followed the veins of silver deep into the rock. That's why it keeps changing direction."

There was another fork—and then another. Each time, Razorback sent one of his shipmates down a different way but, frustratingly, the bosun always managed to pick the same tunnel as Trundle and Esmeralda. Trundle was getting desperately tired. He wasn't used to so much activity and felt as if his poor legs were about to drop off. In the end it was only his terror of the pirates that kept him going, and even then a small part of him just wanted to give up and get it over with. He probably would have done just that if Esmeralda hadn't had such a firm grip on his paw.

Even in such dire straits, Trundle couldn't help noticing that they were coming to parts of the tunnel where there had been rockfalls. Iron rods had been stapled across wide cracks, and wooden props had been hammered in to hold up the roof. They leaped and scrambled over the debris of a dozen old falls.

Only two pirates were now pursuing them as they came to another fork in the tunnel. Please let them both go the other way, Trundle silently begged the Fates as he and Esmeralda dove into the right-hand shaft.

"Abigail Frutch! To the left," echoed Razorback's voice.

Well, good news and bad, thought Trundle. There's only one pirate behind us now—but that pirate happens to be the worst of the lot!

He glanced over his shoulder, seeing the flickering glow of Razorback's torch lighting up the walls behind them.

"Oh!" Esmeralda came to a shuddering halt. They were in a forest of wooden props, hammered into place to hold up the roof—but ahead of them the tunnel had completely collapsed. It was blocked from top to bottom. There was no way forward.

Esmeralda dragged Trundle to one side, closing her fist on the palm light and leaving them in utter, black darkness.

Above the drumming of his blood and the rasp of his breath, Trundle could clearly hear the thunder of Razorback's feet, coming closer and closer. Red torchlight danced along the walls. He peered out from behind a wooden prop. Razorback came careening around the bend, panting and gasping, his tongue lolling and his eyes bulging.

A split second later, Esmeralda leaped out in front of the great hog. She lifted her hand and shouted something that Trundle didn't quite catch, but which sounded like *"Noos-feroo-goo!"* A bolt of bright blue-white lightning shot from her hand and struck the oncoming pirate right between the eyes.

For a few moments Trundle was dazzled by the

light, but as he blinked and his vision cleared, he saw that Razorback was stumbling blindly about with his arms outstretched.

"Ow! Ow! Oww!" Esmeralda was yelling, hopping from foot to foot and shaking her paw as if it were hurting badly.

Trundle's attention was snatched away from her when the pirate's head came in sudden contact with a pitprop. *Clonk!* The impact knocked the prop sideways, and an ominous creaking sounded from above.

"Where are you, you little maggots!" howled Razorback, knuckling his eyes. "When I lay my claws on you—"

The creaking in the roof became a low rumble.

Esmeralda dived to one side, bringing Trundle down with her.

Razorback stared up at the roof. "Curse all hedgchogs!" he shouted.

The low rumbling became a rushing and a roaring

and a tumbling of rock; the air filled with thick coiling and churning smoke. In a sudden mad burst of gallantry, Trundle threw himself on top of Esmeralda to protect her from the roof fall. Small fragments of rock bounced off his back while he waited to be flattened out like a pancake.

At last, the tumultuous noise died away to faint grumbling sounds, and the smoke gradually cleared.

"Get off me, you great lump!" came a stifled voice from beneath Trundle.

He lifted himself to his feet. Small stones and shards fell off him and rattled to the ground. "I was protecting you," he said to Esmeralda as she sat up, puffing and blowing. "That was a noble act!"

"It was indeed, and I thank you for it," she said, lifting her arm to let a new palm light light up the tunnel. She looked around. "Well, that was spectacular! I've never had quite so much success with my fist lightning before." She grimaced. "But it really stings! I hope I don't need to use it too often."

An entire section of the roof had caved in, burying Razorback up to his neck in rubble. His wide-brimmed hat had been staved in, and the magnificent purple feather was reduced to a straggly stem with a few purplish strands hanging off it. The pirate hog's eyes were blissfully closed, and his tongue was hanging out of the side of his snout.

"Is he dead, do you think?" Trundle asked.

"We should be so lucky!" said Esmeralda. "He's just away with the fireflies for a while! Let's get out of here while we still can."

Trundle was about to take her advice when he

noticed something that gleamed white among the gray-and-black wreckage of the roof. "What's that?" he asked, pointing.

"A lump of stone," said Esmeralda. "What else?"

But Trundle wasn't so sure. He climbed across the rubble toward the white thing, gazing at it in awed delight. It was beautiful, shining as though with an inner light.

He picked up the object, feeling it heavy between his paws. He turned, holding it out to Esmeralda, a wide smile breaking across his snout.

"Trundle, you utter genius!" shrieked Esmeralda, her eyes like saucers. "It's the Crystal Crown! You've found the first of the Badgers' Crowns!"

9

THINGS GO BOOM!

Trundle basked for a few moments in Esmeralda's praise.

"Oh, well . . . it was nothing, really," he mumbled humbly. "I simply saw it there, and I said to myself—"

"What's that under your foot?" interrupted Esmeralda. Trundle's moment of glory was over, short-lived but rather pleasant. Esmeralda dived forward and yanked up his foot, pulling something out from beneath it and holding it up to her palm light.

It was a large iron key with a long shaft and intricate teeth. As Esmeralda turned the key in the light, Trundle saw that its oval handle had ornate designs stamped on both faces.

"These are coats of arms," murmured Esmeralda. She frowned. "I don't recognize them, but Aunty will know what they stand for—and most likely she'll also know which lock the key is intended to open." She looked up at Trundle with shining eyes. "We've done it, Lamplighter!" she said jubilantly. "We've found the first crown, Fates be praised." She stood up. "And now we need to get off Drune double quick!"

"I was meaning to ask you about that," Trundle said meaningfully. "How do you suggest we do that, exactly? In case you haven't noticed, the tunnel is blocked in both directions. We're stuck here."

"We'll see about that," Esmeralda said, undaunted. She lifted the paw that held the palm light. "Seek the sun!" she intoned.

"Er, Esmeralda, it's nighttime," Trundle reminded her. "And even if it was daytime, I don't think sunlight would reach this far into Drune."

"Be quiet," said Esmeralda. "You're just embarrassing yourself. This is magic. Watch and learn!"

The little lemon yellow ball of light lifted off Esmeralda's palm. It darted about for a few moments like a sniffer shrew seeking a scent; then, to Trundle's surprise, it shot straight up into the air and disappeared through a hole in the roof, leaving them in total darkness.

"Hey, not so fast! Come back here," called Esmeralda.

The light dropped down again, hovering just above their heads.

Even carrying the crown and the key, it was an easy enough task for Trundle and Esmeralda to clamber over the rubble and push up through the hole in the roof. Trundle had been expecting a long, hard climb, so he was pleasantly surprised when his head popped out into the open and he found himself looking down on the buildings that huddled around the entrance to the mine.

Esmeralda was already on the surface, dusting herself off. The palm light had been extinguished, so the only light now came from the red fires of the braziers burning away below them.

"We'll take one of the skyboats to Rathanger," she told Trundle as he pulled himself up out of the hole. "The sooner we're away from here, the better. With luck, there'll be a windship leaving Rathanger soon. We'll sneak aboard and let the Fates take us to our next port of call."

"Er, excuse me," said Trundle. "Two things. First, what about the slaves? Second, what do you mean by 'next port of call'?"

"I told you before, there's nothing we can do for the slaves," Esmeralda replied. "It's sad, but there it is.

And as for the rest—you seem to forget that there are still five crowns to find. We've hardly even started!"

"But I promised those poor creatures we'd try to help them," Trundle objected.

"I know you did." Esmeralda was already making her way down the hillside. "I thought it was a mistake at the time."

Feeling disgruntled and faithless, Trundle trailed after Esmeralda, the shining crystal crown tucked safely under his arm. They came down among the sheds and shacks. There was no one in sight, but from a nearby warehouse they could hear raised voices; among them, Trundle could make out that of Mr. Pouncepot.

"A tankard of ale is just the thing to quench the thirst after hard labor!" he was announcing loudly. "Half the cargo is unloaded, and we deserve a breather before we shift the rest."

"Since when did you become an acquaintance of hard labor, Mr. Pouncepot?" roared another familiar voice, to harsh laughter and cheery jeers. "Unless looking on while others sweat makes you weary!" It was the voice of Overseer Grunther.

"That takes its toll, Mistress Grunther," cackled Mr. Pouncepot. "That surely takes its toll!"

There was another burst of laughter and shouts for more ale. Clearly, the windship's crew and a gang of mine guards were enjoying some liquid refreshment in the warehouse to help their work along.

"I hear there's a spot of trouble in the mines," declared Mr. Pouncepot. "Runaways running rampant and the slaves threatening rebellion."

"The runaways are Razorback's problem," replied Grunther genially. "And I'll soon quiet them slaves down. I'll put a few of the ringleaders' feet to the fires—that'll learn 'em!"

Trundle shivered at the thought of those sad animals being tortured by that horrible hog. He turned to whisper something to Esmeralda, but found that she had crept away and was on the far side of the jetty, checking out the skyboats. He was shocked by the fact that she didn't seem to care about the slaves. She of all people should know what vile lives they were forced to live. She *should* do something to help!

He padded softly across the jetty, meaning to have a stern word with her. At heart, he was sure she was a good creature—she just needed a little prod now and then.

"This one looks a trim little craft," Esmeralda said, pointing to one of the skyboats. Like all the other vessels, it had a propeller at its stern attached to a seat with a mechanical treadle device. Trundle assumed that when there was no wind to fill the sail, someone would sit there and pedal away like mad to turn the propeller and move the skyboat forward.

"Hop aboard," said Esmeralda. "I'll untie her. Then off we go!"

"No," Trundle said firmly. "We're doing no such thing. We're going to help the slaves."

Esmeralda turned and eyed him, folding her arms. "How?" she said. "Just tell me exactly how you plan on us helping the slaves."

"I don't know," Trundle admitted. "But we must. We have to! That Grunther woman is talking about burning their feet!" He turned and began to walk back toward the mines. "You don't have to come."

"Then give me the crown!" Esmeralda demanded. "If you're dead set on getting yourself killed, or worse, at least don't let the Badgers' Crystal Crown fall into enemy hands!"

Trundle stopped, quivering with indignation. "Is that all you care about?" he asked. "The blessed crown?"

Esmeralda marched up to him, her arms outstretched. "At the moment, yes!" she said, trying to snatch the crown from under his arm.

Trundle stepped back, clutching the crown to himself. "No!" he said. "I found it. You're not getting it!"

"Don't be an idiot!"

"At least I'm not a heartless brute!"

She lunged for the crown, but he leaped back, hitting his shoulder against something hard and hot.

"Trundle! Careful!" gasped Esmeralda, as he stumbled over the leg of one of the iron braziers. The brazier toppled over, spilling burning coals across the jetty.

"Now look what you made me do!" hissed Trundle, glancing anxiously toward the half-closed doors of the warehouse where Mr. Pouncepot and Overseer Grunther and the rest were carousing.

A sharp spitting, spluttering, crackling sound came to his ears. Esmeralda was staring openmouthed at the boards of the jetty, where a bright white sparking fire was suddenly burning among the red coals of the braziers. As they watched, the sparky white fire divided into two channels that went running off in

opposite directions, following a black line that he had not noticed before.

The black line led the length of the jetty—from the gangplank of the windship at one end, all the way in through the warehouse doors at the other.

"Uh, Trundle," said Esmeralda, looking first at the windship and then up to the warehouse. "How firmly did you put the bung back in that barrel of blackpowder you were messing with on the way here?"

"I'm not sure," Trundle admitted. "Why?"

Esmeralda pointed to the snaking black thread. The two bright little fires were zooming along at great speed now, one heading for the windship, the other making its rapid way to the warehouse.

"Because I think the bung came out again while they were unloading the barrel," Esmeralda said. "And I think the blackpowder spilled out. And if some of the barrels are still on the windship, then the windship is about to blow up. And if the rest of the barrels are in that warehouse—"

She didn't need to finish the sentence.

"Oh!" said Trundle as he watched the skittering ball of sparks zoom in through the gap between the warehouse doors. "I see."

A puzzled voice sounded above the hubbub in the warehouse. "What's that?"

"What's what?" asked another voice.

"The burning thing coming toward the barrel you're sitting on."

"Oh, *that*. Well, offhand, I'd say it was—"

KA-BOOM!

Trundle and Esmeralda were blown clean off their feet by the blast. Trundle lay flat on his back, his ears ringing and his whiskers singed, watching a huge bloom of red smoke go boiling up into the air. A second or two later, shards of splintered wood and a sprinkling of glass fragments and pieces of metal and other stuff that went

splat, came raining down. Trundle preferred not to look

at the splats. He had a nasty feeling he already knew what

they were: sticky little remnants of exploded windship

crew and mine guards.

Esmeralda got up and tottered over to Trundle to

help him to his feet.

"Look what you did!" she shouted in his ear.

"Beg pardon?" he shouted back, his whole head

ringing with a thousand tinny bells.

"I was just saying—" Esmeralda began at high volume. But before she could finish, something came crashing down at Trundle's feet. He leaped back in shock. It was a wide leather belt, studded with iron hooks from which hung an assortment of keys.

A moment later, something roundish whacked down on the boards nearby and went bounding along the jetty.

"Don't look!" warned Esmeralda. "I think that was Grunther's head!"

But Trundle was far more interested in the singed and smoking belt. He picked it up and hung it around his neck, the keys jingling.

He looked at Esmeralda. "Now can we go and help the slaves?" he asked, drawing his sword.

"You bet!" she laughed. "Lead on, Trundle, my lad!"

HOMEWARD BOUND?

Trundle and Esmeralda ran into the main entrance of the mines. A scene of complete pandemonium met them. Guards were running this way and that, wielding their whips and yelling for the slaves to behave themselves.

The enslaved animals were having none of it! It was as if the explosion had ignited a new and fierce spirit in them. Despite their chains, and despite being tired and worn down and weak from hunger and overwork, the slaves were revolting! Some were up on the terraces, pelting the guards with lumps of coal. Others had surrounded their captors and were giving them a thorough pummeling, while yet another group was charging about with a ladder held between them, using it as a very effective battering ram to fell any guard who got in their way.

Esmeralda scooped up a pickax and raced to join in the fray, while Trundle, sword in hand to be on the safe side, put his best efforts into finding the right key for the right padlock on every set of slaves' chains.

It didn't take long for Trundle to do his work. Soon all the prisoners were free and all the guards were either stretched unconscious on the ground or herded together and fettered by their own chains. The liberated animals came swarming around Esmeralda and Trundle, cheering and shouting for joy.

"Quiet, please! Quiet!" howled Esmeralda. "We don't have time for a barn dance! As soon as word gets to Rathanger of what's happened in the mine, they'll send more guards to put down the rebellion. We need to get out of here!"

"To the skyboats!" shouted a voice.

"To the skyboats!" echoed dozens of other voices, and moments later all the slaves were streaming from the cavern and heading for the jetty.

Suddenly Esmeralda and Trundle found themselves quite alone in the mine. Trundle was feeling a little dazed by what had happened.

"We did well!" grinned Esmeralda. "And you *did* manage to free them, you resourceful hedgehog, you!"

"I couldn't have done it on my own," replied Trundle, which was perfectly true. "And I'm sorry I called you a heartless brute."

"Don't mention it," said Esmeralda.

Trundle frowned at her. "This is where you apologize for calling me an idiot," he pointed out.

Esmeralda gave a merry laugh. "But you *are* an

idiot, Trundle," she chuckled. "The bestest, bravest, smartest, luckiest idiot I ever did meet!"

"All right, then . . . apology accepted," said Trundle. He looked out through the mine entrance. "I hope they all get away."

"Lawks!" hollered Esmeralda. "Never mind them—what about *us*? All the skyboats will be gone!"

They bolted for the open air. A marvelous, heart-lifting sight met their eyes. All along the dark length of the jetty, skyboats full of jubilant ex-slaves were casting off their moorings and rising into the air.

"Oh, crikey!" wailed Trundle as he realized that almost all the vessels had already moved away out of reach.

The leading skyboats were now turning and gliding off along the chasm toward the distant lights of Rathanger, their propellers whirring as they moved swiftly through the dark air like a school of slender fish.

Trundle and Esmeralda pelted along the jetty. "Wait!" Esmeralda yelled, waving her arms. "Wait for us!"

But the buzzing of the propellers was like a swarm of angry bees, and her voice was lost in the noise.

"Look!" gasped Trundle, pointing to the very last skyboat that was still attached to the jetty. Its name was written in silver leaf on the bows: the *Thief in the Night*.

A solitary figure was straining and tugging at the rope that held the skyboat up against its moorings. It was a bedraggled squirrel. He stared at them with bright, worried eyes as they came hurtling toward him.

"I can't get the knots free!" he called.

"Allow me!" said Trundle, bringing his sword down with all his strength on the knotted rope.

The blade cut through the knot. At once, the squirrel leaped into the skyboat, plumped himself down in the mechanical seat, and started pounding away at the treadles with both feet.

Esmeralda jumped in just as the skyboat started

to move away from the jetty. Trundle hesitated for a second as the gap grew, then flung himself headlong into the bottom of the vessel. Even before he got himself untangled and sat up, their skyboat had risen high above the jetty and caught up with the last few stragglers as they sped to freedom. He and Esmeralda had made it in the nick of time!

The squirrel was singing at the top of his voice as he pedaled away in the stern of the skyboat.

Sing ho! For the open skyway,
Sing ho! For the open sky!
With a yo-ho-ho, and a yodel-dee-doh,
We're off to distant islands-o!

Trundle and Esmeralda looked at each other and laughed.

The squirrel paused in his singing and gave them the widest grin they had ever seen. "The name's Jack

Nimble," he said. "At your service, my fine friends! Traveling troubadour, minstrel, and bard by trade."

"I'm Esmeralda, and this is Trundle," said Esmeralda.

"Well, hello to the both of you," said Jack. "Do you by any chance have a sunder for a song upon you? It's been an age since last I performed a ditty, and I'm so full of music I think I might just burst clean out of my skin!"

And he began to sing again, his voice soaring as his knees pumped up and down and the propeller spun and the swift little vessel zipped along.

There was a brisk young weasel
Who did a-wooing go!
But he found himself at the bar of an inn
And that weasel just couldn't say no, ho-ho,
Oh, that weasel could never say no. . . .

While he sang, the flotilla of skyboats flew over Rathanger. The escapees shouted and waved merrily down at the verminous creatures who stared angrily up at them, shaking fists and clubs and calling out terrible oaths and curses as they flashed by.

Esmeralda leaned out over the bow. "Look! Trundle! There's the *Iron Pig* with its sails furled and its decks empty! Ha ha! While Grizzletusk's brigands are getting soused in the Strangled Stoat, we fly away like birds!" She leaned farther out, yelling rude comments down at the ironclad pirate ship.

"Careful," warned Trundle, catching hold of her belt to save her from toppling out of the little vessel.

She pulled herself back, her eyes shining. "We beat 'em, Trundle! We totally beat 'em!"

"Yes, we did!" laughed Trundle.

Once they were out in the open and clear of Drune, the skyboats began to dart off every which way into the star-filled night.

"So?" said Jack. "Where are we going, my fine

fellows? I know of a delightful little hostelry out near Dangler's Calm where we'll receive a hearty welcome. Or we could go to Willowland or Swiveltree or Port Trimble or anywhere else you might fancy in all the wide worlds! You choose— I'm easy!"

"I'd like to go home," Trundle said.

"And where might that be?" beamed Jack.

"Shiverstones," said Trundle.

Jack Nimble gave a visible shudder. "Cabbages and cabbages and more cabbages," he said. "Choose again, for pity's sake."

"Actually, we're on a quest," said Esmeralda.

Jack smacked his paws together, his eyes gleaming. "That sounds more like it!" he said. "A quest for what, pray? Not cabbages, I hope."

"We're looking for the Six Crowns of the Badgers of Power," said Esmeralda.

Trundle half expected Jack to burst out laughing, but he didn't. "Is that so?" he said. "Hmm. Interesting. And unless I'm much mistaken, that there shiny thingamajig would be the first of them," he added, pointing to the Crystal Crown that was still tucked under Trundle's arm. "So? Where are the others?"

"We don't know," said Trundle.

"But we found this with it," said Esmeralda, pulling the key out of a fold of her dress and holding it up. "We'll have to ask my aunty about that. She's the queen of the Roamanys and by far the cleverest person in the whole of the Sundered Lands."

"And she'll tell us where the next crown is and what mysterious lock the key will open!" shouted Jack. "A most excellent plan! And what a worthy enterprise!"

Trundle looked from Esmeralda to Jack Nimble. He did rather want to go home. He felt that he'd played his part and was due a nice long rest. But any hope he had that Jack might be a sensible, level-headed animal who would help him convince the crazy Roamany girl to forget about the crowns evaporated as he saw the light of new adventure shining in their eyes.

"All right," sighed Trundle. "Have it your way. Let's find your aunty."

And let's hope she puts a stop to all this gallivanting and takes me home! he said secretly to himself.

"Where shall we find the queen of the Roamanys?" asked Jack.

"I'll have to think about that," said Esmeralda. She stood up and began to unfurl the sail. They would no longer need pedal power now that they were out among the winds of the Sundered Lands. She glanced back the way they had come. "Uh-oh!"

"Now what?" sighed Trundle.

"Look!"

The three animals turned to look back toward

Drune. A windship was sailing out of the gaping mouth of the Rathanger chasm. A large windship, bristling with cannon. An ironclad windship with billowing bloodred sails.

"The *Iron Pig*," groaned Trundle.

"Oh, heck!" exclaimed Jack.

"Help me hoist the sail," shouted Esmeralda. "Maybe we can outrun them!"

Trundle looked anxiously back as the sails of the pirate windship caught the breeze and filled to bursting.

"*Can* we outrun them?" he asked uneasily.

Esmeralda grinned wildly at him. "Let's find out!"

A moment later, the sail was unfurled and the yellow canvas caught the wind, and the little skyboat went skimming away across the dark star-strewn heavens like an arrow from the bow.